PRISCILLA TADPOLE

By Gwen Costello

Illustrated by Maryann Read

ty-Third Publications
illow Street
ox 180
, CT 06355
536-2611 • (800) 321-0411

0-89622-527-5

Not so very long ago, there were two little tadpoles
named Priscilla and Harvey
who lived in Glover Pond.

They were the best of friends
and spent many happy hours together.
From sunup to sunset
they swam and played without a care.

For them, being a tadpole
was the best thing in the world.

They thought the only creatures in Glover Pond
were other tadpoles, fish,
and a nasty old snapping turtle named Rufus.
Their world was very small
but they liked it that way.

One morning, when Priscilla looked for Harvey,
she couldn't find him.
"He's probably swimming
at the other end of Glover Pond," she said,
and decided to swim alone.

She swam as fast as she could,
up toward the top of the pond,
and then down toward the bottom.

Up and down she went, faster and faster.
Priscilla didn't realize that every time
she swam to the surface
she was bumping into a lily pad.

On that lily pad sat a big old frog named Bella,
and the little tadpole had disturbed her nap.
"Hey! What's going on down there?"
the sleepy frog called out.

Priscilla was frightened by the voice,
and stared up at the strange-looking creature.

Finally, Priscilla asked,
"What sort of fish are you?"
The old frog laughed with delight.
"Why, I'm not a fish," Bella said; "I'm a frog!
I was once a tadpole like you,
but all tadpoles become frogs, just like me."

"Oh, no!" Priscilla cried, "I don't want to be a frog.
I'm happy being me!
I don't want to be anything else."
She got so upset that she didn't notice Rufus
sneaking up on her, hoping to eat her for lunch!

But Bella could see Rufus, with his mouth wide open,
getting closer and closer to Priscilla.
"Watch out, little tadpole!" she called.

It was a close call,
but Priscilla got away just in time.

She was grateful to Bella,
but she was still afraid
of becoming a frog.
"There must be some mistake,"
she thought as she swam away.
"I won't change, I just won't!"

When Priscilla finally stopped swimming
she heard a voice calling, "Cilla, Cilla."
Only Harvey used that name!

But when she looked up,
all she saw was a frog.
Priscilla couldn't believe her eyes.
Could it be?
Had Harvey become a frog?

Harvey could tell that Priscilla was upset.
He told her how much he liked being a frog.
"You're still my best friend, Cilla," he said.
"We can still do lots of things together,
especially when you become a frog, too!"

Priscilla wouldn't hear any of it.
She simply would not become a frog—
even for Harvey.

But no matter how hard she tried,
changes kept happening to Priscilla.
She started growing legs and arms,
and her body was turning green.

As she noticed each new change,
she tried very hard to keep it from happening.
She didn't want to change.
She wanted to be a tadpole forever.

In spite of all her efforts, Priscilla was almost a frog.

But guess what?

She soon discovered that frogs could do lots of things

that a tadpole just could not.

As a tadpole,

Priscilla had to stay underwater to breathe.

Now she could jump out of the pond onto a lily pad—

and still breathe.

As a frog, Priscilla could make strange new sounds,
and even jump from one log to another
without worrying about Rufus.

One day while she sat in the sun on a lily pad,
Priscilla felt a thump under her feet.
She looked down and saw a tiny tadpole
swimming up and down, up and down,
playing a game against the lily pad.

Priscilla looked down and said, "Hello! "
The startled tadpole cried out,
"What kind of fish are you?"

Priscilla laughed.
Not so long ago, she had asked the same question herself.
"Now, now," Priscilla said, "don't be afraid.
Frogs look big and strange to little tadpoles.
I know, because I was once a tadpole like you."

"I thought that being a tadpole
was the best thing in the world," Priscilla continued.
"But there's so much more to do and see
when you're a frog."

Priscilla then explained that all tadpoles change
and gradually become frogs.
When she finished, the little tadpole
was excited about becoming a frog.

As the little tadpole swam away,
Priscilla realized
that one of the best things about being a frog
was helping tadpoles not to be afraid of change.

She smiled as she remembered
how she had not wanted to become a frog.
"It was fun being a tadpole," she said to herself,
"but it's much more exciting being a frog."

Ask your children how they feel about change. Do they remember what it was like to be very young? How are they different from the way they were last year, or the year before?

Have they ever had to move from one place to another, make new friends, go to a new school? Have them describe the experience. Talk about some of the good things that happen with change, as well as some of the scary things they might feel.